Dedicated to all the Frontline Heroes
&
Resilient Children of 2020

ISBN: 978-1-7775303-5-8
(Hardcover Book)

Hearts Full of Hope/ Meera Bala, "Hearts Full of Hope" follows five kids around the world as they do their part to save lives just by staying home

Editing and Proofreading by Tania Barlow
Illustration by Aldi Mustofa

Printed in Canada
First Printed in April 2021

Published by MB Publishing

www.wordsbymeera.com
@wordsby.meera

Hearts Full of Hope

Aiden Ming Vani Sulo Bruno

Writen by Meera Bala   **Illustrated by Aldi Mustofa**

On a beautiful spring day, the world shut down. We all stayed home because of a virus that made people sick.

We started virtual school. The teachers
sang and danced to cheer us up.

Dad worked from home. He cooked, cleaned,
and fixed our Wi-Fi connection.

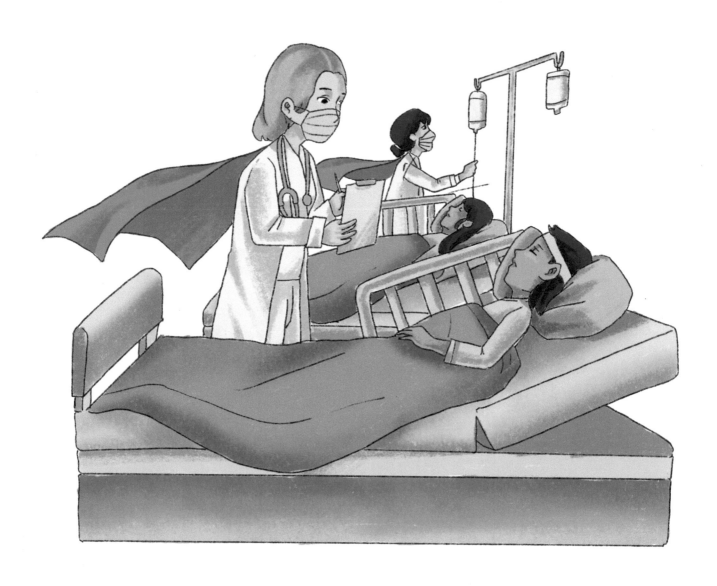

Mom turned into a superhero at the hospital.
Doctors and nurses worked night and day to help
those who were sick.

To keep them safe from the virus, Grandpa and
Grandma couldn't visit anymore. We gave them
kisses through the phone.

We played board games. We read books.
We played video games too.

When my dad went to get groceries, he wore a mask.
We sent thank-you cards with him for all the essential
workers.

We made healthy meals at home.
Of course, we baked banana bread.

We went for hikes. We rode our bikes.
We discovered trails in our neighborhood.

We saw animals roaming freely. They enjoyed
the freedom of our quieter streets.

We exercised. We meditated. We prayed.

We worried. We cried.

We hugged our family tightly.

We thanked the frontline workers who go out
to keep us safe.

We stayed home to protect our grandparents,
doctors, and each other.

Our hearts are full of hope.

If we all work together, the world will rise again!

About the Author

Meera Bala is a Tamil-Canadian author and publisher of children's books. She graduated from York University's Concurrent Education Program with a Bachelor of Education and Bachelor of Arts (Hons) in English. As an elementary school teacher, she enjoys sharing her love of reading and writing with her students. Her first book, *Palm Tress Under Snow* is based on Meera Bala's own experience of immigrating from Sri Lanka to Canada in the 1980s. Meera Bala's mission is to write books that represent diversity and inclusion and also empowers and inspires children. She lives in Ontario, Canada with her loving husband and two wonderful sons. When she's not writing or teaching, you can find her relaxing with a cup of coffee and a good book in a sunny location.

www.wordsbymeera.com
@wordsby.meera

CPSIA information can be obtained
at www.ICGtesting.com
Printed in the USA
BVHW020826220421
605420BV00008B/4